Imagine That!

Yasmeen Ismail

BLOOMSBURY

NEW YORK LONDON OXFORD NEW DELHI SYDNEY

"Lila,
have you put your
shoes on yet?"

"Lila?"

"Lila, what *are* you doing?"

Nothing...

I'll fight this *fearsome* monster
and soon he will **regret**
not *giving up* much sooner to
become my faithful **pet** . . .

"Lila, have you put
your **coat** on?

Grandpa will
be waiting!"

"What's going **on**
over there?"

FLIP and spring and ZOOM and tumble,

I won't slip, I NEVER fumble!

I boing and bounce!
I ping and pong!

I'm quick and swift
and super STRONG!

"Okay, let's get going . . ."

RARRR-RRR!

Giants are the LOUDEST of all.

We're BIG and strong and very tall.

Fee–Fi–Fo and Fum!

You'd better hide before I come.

"Lila . . .

LILA!
Slow down!

What are
you *doing?*"

TRASH

MAIL

Nothing...

I am the queen of super speed!
Nothing can stop these noble steeds.

I'll CRASH down mountains and tear through trees!

You'll NEVER catch up with meeeee . . .

"Lila, look at you!
Are you getting taller?"

"What have you been doing
since I last saw you?"

Nothing...

I'm very busy all the time,
with things to **see** and trees to **climb**.

Up and **up**, right to the sky,

to wave at birds,
as they *fly by.*

"Who are you
waving to, Lila?"

"Lila?"

Oh, Grandpa,
*can't you **see**?*
*I was **sitting***
*in that **tree** . . .*

And like the birds, I'll *fly away* . . .

I don't suppose **you** could _follow_ me?

Watch out, Lila! Here I come!
I too can play pretend!
There's really **nothing** to it . . .

It's SO much better with a friend!

For Lila
(Max and Spiderman)

First published in Great Britain in August 2016 by Bloomsbury Publishing Plc
Published in the United States of America in July 2017 by Bloomsbury Children's Books
www.bloomsbury.com

Bloomsbury is a registered trademark of Bloomsbury Publishing Plc

For information about permission to reproduce selections from this book, write to
Permissions, Bloomsbury Children's Books, 1385 Broadway, New York, New York 10018
Bloomsbury books may be purchased for business or promotional use. For information on bulk purchases
please contact Macmillan Corporate and Premium Sales Department at specialmarkets@macmillan.com

Library of Congress Cataloging-in-Publication Data
Names: Ismail, Yasmeen, author, illustrator.
Title: Imagine that! / by Yasmeen Ismail.
Description: New York : Bloomsbury, [2017]
Summary: Mommy and Lila are going to visit Grandpa, but Lila is busy playing in her own imaginary world.
Grandpa decides to join Lila—because using your imagination is even more fun when you play together!
Identifiers: LCCN 2016032053
ISBN 978-1-68119-362-5 (hardcover) • ISBN 978-1-68119-726-5 (e-book) • ISBN 978-1-68119-727-2 (e-PDF)
Subjects: | CYAC: Stories in rhyme. | Imagination—Fiction. | Play—Fiction. | Grandfathers—Fiction. | BISAC: JUVENILE FICTION / Imagination & Play. |
JUVENILE FICTION / Family / General (see also headings under Social Issues). | JUVENILE FICTION / Girls & Women.
Classification: LCC PZ8.3.I786 Im 2017 | DDC [E]—dc23
LC record available at https://lccn.loc.gov/2016032053

Art created with watercolors • Typeset in Usherwood Medium and hand lettering • Book design by Goldy Broad
Printed in China by Leo Paper Products, Heshan, Guangdong
2 4 6 8 10 9 7 5 3 1

All papers used by Bloomsbury Publishing, Inc., are natural, recyclable products made from wood grown in well-managed forests.
The manufacturing processes conform to the environmental regulations of the country of origin.